Disney · PIXAR
COCO

Level 3

Re-told by: Mo Sanders
Series Editor: Rachel Wilson

Pearson Education Limited
KAO Two
KAO Park, Harlow,
Essex, CMI7 9NA, England
and Associated Companies throughout the world.

ISBN: 978-1-2923-4678-6

This edition first published by Pearson Education Ltd 2020

1 3 5 7 9 10 8 6 4 2

Set in Heinemann Roman Special, 14pt/23pt
Printed by Neografia, Slovakia

Published by Pearson Education Limited

Acknowledgments
123RF.com: artush 22, Jose de Jesus Churion Del Vecchio 23
Alamy Stock Photo: Richard Ellis 27
Getty Images: ABIDAL 23, Dhananjaya Bandara JM / 500px 24, Sollina Images 22,
©Studio One-One 24, tylim 22
Shutterstock.com: Dina Julayeva 26, JuanSalvador 24, Julia Pavaliuk 23, Leon Rafael 24

For a complete list of the titles available in the Pearson English Readers series, visit
www.pearsonenglishreaders.com.

Alternatively, write to your local Pearson Education office or
to Pearson English Readers Marketing Department,
Pearson Education, KAO Two, KAO Park, Harlow, Essex, CMI7 9NA

In This Book

Miguel

A Mexican boy with a big family and a guitar

Abuelita

Miguel's grandmother

Coco

Abuelita's mother

Ernesto de la Cruz

A singer with many famous songs

Mamá Imelda

Coco's dead mother

Hector

A dead musician

Before You Read

Introduction

Miguel wants to play in a music competition, but his family hates music. He takes the guitar of a famous singer. Suddenly, he goes to a strange world and meets his family … his *dead* family! Can he find a way back to *his* world?

Activities

1 **Look at the pictures in the book and choose the right answers.**

1 What is Miguel doing on page 3?
  a listening to music
  b dancing
  c playing the guitar

2 What is he doing on page 12?
  a putting paint on his face
  b looking at his face
  c washing his face

2 **Match the words to the sentences. You can use a dictionary.**

promise poison disappear competition

1 "I can't see it!"
2 "I want to play in this."
3 "Do not drink it!"
4 "Please do this for me."

Coco's family loved to sing and dance.

But Coco's father wanted to play his music to all the world.

He said goodbye, and Coco didn't see him again.

Many years later, Coco was *very* old.

Coco's daughter was Miguel's grandmother, Abuelita. Abuelita remembered her mother's sad story and she always shouted, "*No music!*"

For a long time, there was no music in the Rivera home.

But Miguel was different …

Miguel loved music. His favorite musician was Ernesto de la Cruz. Ernesto was dead now, but Miguel loved to play all the songs from the singer's movies.

Today was the Día de los Muertos, or the Day of the Dead. And tonight, there was a music competition in town. Miguel wanted to go.

The Día de los Muertos was an important day. People liked
to remember their families. There was a table with old family
photographs, flowers, bread, fruit, and more.
Food! Miguel's dog Dante wanted some, but . . . *CRASH!*

Miguel looked down at the old photograph of Coco's family. Her father's face wasn't there, but there was a guitar with a skull on it! Ernesto de la Cruz's guitar!

Was it true? Was Ernesto the musician in Miguel's family?

"SEIZE YOUR MOMENT!"

"Mamá Coco's father was Ernesto de la Cruz!" Miguel shouted.

"I can be a musician, too!"

Abuelita was angry. She smashed Miguel's guitar.

"No!" Miguel cried, "I don't want to be in this family!"

He ran into town.

Now Miguel didn't have a guitar for the competition.
But Ernesto's guitar was on the wall inside the singer's tomb.
"Please don't be angry," Miguel said. "I'm only taking this for the competition."
Suddenly, there was a beautiful light in the tomb.

Afraid, Miguel started to run. "What's happening?"
His parents were outside, but they didn't see Miguel.
They walked *through* him.
There were skeletons all around Miguel. On Día de los
Muertos they were back to visit their families!

The dead Riveras were back, also. They were very surprised
to see Miguel. Why was he in their world?
They wanted to ask Mamá Imelda about this. They asked
Miguel to follow them across the bridge of flowers.

Mamá Imelda, Coco's mother, was there.

"I can send you back to your world," she said. "But you have to promise one thing. NO MORE MUSIC!"

"What? No way!" Miguel thought. "I can't promise that!"

Outside, there was a skeleton called Hector.
"I'm looking for Ernesto de la Cruz," Miguel said. "He's the
only person from my family here."
"I know him," Hector said. "I can help you, and later you can
help me."

Hector started to put skeleton face paint on Miguel.
"Listen," he said. "I'm slowly disappearing because people
in your world are forgetting me. But you can change that."
He showed Miguel an old photo.

"So, you get me to Ernesto, then I put up your photo
back home?" asked Miguel.

"What a smart boy! Yes!" Hector said.

Miguel and Hector talked to some musicians.
"There's that music competition," said one of them. "The people's favorite singer can play at Ernesto's party."
Miguel was excited, but on stage he was afraid, also. Then Hector started to dance and Miguel played.
The skeletons loved them!

Suddenly, the Riveras were there and they wanted Miguel.
All the skeletons looked for him, but Miguel ran fast.
"You DO have more family!" Hector cried. "I'm taking you
to them."
"You don't want to help me!" Miguel shouted. He walked
away.

Miguel arrived at the party. He was excited to meet Ernesto.
"I'm Miguel. Your great-great grandson," he said. "With your
help, I can go home and be a musician, too."
Ernesto was very happy about this.

Suddenly, Hector was there.

"Miguel, you promised to take my photo back with you!"
he shouted.

"Hector?" Ernesto looked at the skeleton. "You're
disappearing."

"Why's that?" Hector cried angrily. "You're famous, but those
were *my* songs!"

"What?" Miguel said.

It was true: Ernesto didn't write his songs. It was Hector!
And Hector, not Ernesto, was Coco's father.
"You poisoned me, Ernesto!" Hector said. "I only wanted
to go home."
Miguel stayed with Hector. "He's disappearing fast,"
he thought.

Later, Imelda helped them. She wasn't angry now because it was true—Ernesto poisoned her husband. Music wasn't bad— *Ernesto* was bad!

"There's no more time …" Hector said weakly.

"No!" cried Miguel. "Coco can't forget you!"

Imelda and Hector smiled at him with love.

"Go home, Miguel," Hector said.

"And play your music," Imelda said kindly.

And then … *WHOOSH!*

Miguel was back in his world! He started to run.

At home, he played a song for Mamá Coco.

"Miguel, STOP!" Abuelita cried.

But Mamá Coco smiled. "That's my papa's song," she said,
and she showed them an old photo of her father—Hector!

She remembered him!

Now, there's always music in Miguel's home, and on Día de los Muertos *all* the Riveras enjoy it.

After You Read

1   **Match the names to the sentences.**

> Abuelita   Coco   Ernesto   Hector

1 Her father didn't come home.
2 He poisoned his friend.
3 He was Imelda's husband.
4 She always shouts, "No music!" at Miguel.

2   **Choose the correct answers.**

1 In the tomb, why does Miguel take Ernesto's guitar?
  a He wants to play it in the competition.
  b He wants to take it over the flower bridge.
  c He wants to take it home.

2 Why did Hector never come home?
  a His friend poisoned him.
  b He wanted to be famous.
  c He didn't like his family.

3   **How are these things different one year later? Discuss the questions.**

1 What does Abuelita think about music?
2 What do people think about Ernesto?
3 Who starts to visit the Riveras every Día de los Muertos?

Picture Dictionary

bridge

face paint

forget

guitar

musicians

photograph

singer

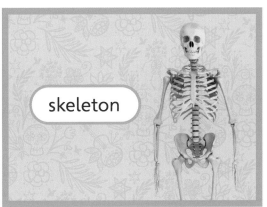

skeleton

skull

smash

stage

tomb

Phonics

Say the sounds. Read the words.

sk
sm

(skull)   (smile)

fl
pl

(flower)   (play)

br
dr

(bread)   (dress)

Say the rhyme.

Miguel walked back from that beautiful place
With a song in his head and a smile on his face.
Across the flower bridge to see
His grandmother and his family.
The skeletons all look down and say,
"That boy can sing, that boy can play!"

Values

Believe in your abilities.

Oh ...

Are you always afraid before you go on stage?

I don't know. This is my first time.

You can *DO* this! Go out there and show them. But first give me a good, loud shout. Listen ...

OOOOOOOOH HE-HE-HEY!

Find Out

What happens on Día de los Muertos?

In Mexico on November 1st and 2nd, many people celebrate the Día de los Muertos. This is a happy time for families to remember dead people.
In Mexico City there's a big parade with a lot of costumes and music.

pattern

costume

On Día de los Muertos ...

- Orange flowers show the way back to this world.
- The dead people are hungry and thirsty on their one day back in our world. Their families put favorite foods and drinks on shrines for them.
- There are skeletons and skulls with flower patterns.
- Children often eat candy skulls.

shrine

candy

27